Dream Big
and be
Yourself

**Inspiring Stories for Girls about Self-Esteem,
Confidence, Courage, and Friendship**

Nadia Ross

Special Art Stories

Dream Big and Be Yourself

Inspiring Stories for Girls about Self-Esteem, Confidence, Courage, and Friendship

Nadia Ross

Paperback ISBN: 979-12-80592-36-1
support@specialartbooks.com
www.specialartbooks.com

Table of Contents

Introduction

Hello Amazing Girl! Do you know how many different people there are in the world?

Every person has dreams and different ways to achieve their goals. There will be times when you want to accomplish your dreams but don't think you can do it. Don't listen to those thoughts. You are more capable and able than you realize. Be confident in yourself and continue through challenges and hardships.

This book will introduce you to a group of girls who go through the same things you do every day. They are scared, worried, and sometimes, they don't win right away. They work hard, learn from mistakes, and keep trying. These girls get discouraged, doubt their abilities, and sometimes they almost give up, but somewhere deep inside of them, their light shines through. They find their courage and self-confidence and push through their difficult moments to reach their dreams and goals.

When you learn to be yourself and find pride in what you do, everything you want to happen can become a reality. You are an amazing girl! You can do everything you want and even more than you ever thought. Keep reaching for your dreams

4

every day! Before you know it, those dreams will become a reality, opening up your life for more dreams, challenges, and growth.

Tae Speaks Two Languages

Each person comes from a different place. Some people speak other languages you may not know. There are times when these languages may sound a little strange, but when you listen closely, you can hear how beautiful they are. If you ask, you may even learn something new. When you broaden your horizons, whether over languages, heritage, or culture, you get a chance to see how much bigger the world is and discover how wonderful other viewpoints really are.

6

Even when you are the one who feels different, know that you have something amazing to offer the world. You can help others see things in a new way, enriching their lives with incredible warmth and a better understanding of who you are.

What differences do you think you have? How can you share your special gifts with the rest of the world?

Tae is a girl who speaks two languages. She loves them both but doesn't feel like she can share them. What do you think happens when someone overhears her using her first language?

~ ~ ~

As Tae got ready to go to school, nervousness tickled her belly like it was full of butterflies. It wasn't a new feeling, but she was bothered by it all the same. Each day, when she was inside her house, she felt warm and comfortable. But when she left her home she sometimes felt sad, like she was leaving part of herself behind.

In a way, she was.

Tae spoke two languages and she knew that her classmates did not speak her native language: Mandarin Chinese. So, when she was in school, she didn't feel she could be her full self.

She slid her backpack on, looked over her shoulder, and called, "Zài jiàn!" (goodbye!) to her mother and grandmother, who were in the kitchen getting ready to start their day.

Tae walked out the door and down to the end of her driveway. While waiting for the bus, she sang the English version of the alphabet to remind herself of what it was. After she got to school, she sat quietly with her hands folded and waited for class to start.

"Hi, Tae," a girl named Becky said as she slid into the desk next to Tae.

Tae smiled and softly said, "Hello." Tae thought that Becky was nice. Her bright red hair was long, curly, and very different from Tae's, whose black hair was very straight and short. Becky always tried to get Tae to sit with her at lunch and play with her during breaks. Tae always appreciated it.

As class began, Tae sat back and watched the other students answer the teacher's questions. While she knew her English was good, she still felt too shy to answer. Even though she knew the answers to most of the questions, she didn't feel comfortable speaking out.

Once the teacher finished their reading subject, she handed out a math pop quiz. Tae looked at the numbers on the page, and, although they were familiar, anxiety built up in her chest because she was never very good at being put on the spot.

Tae reached into her desk to pull out her pencil case, and her nerves got the best of her. Instead of grabbing the edge of the case, she missed. As she pulled her arm back out, her sleeve caught on the zipper. She tried to jerk it away but, instead, the case flew into her lap and spilled her pencils and erasers all over the floor in a big CRASH!

Every head in class whipped toward her and her cheeks flushed with embarrassment.

Tae cast her eyes down and whispered, "Tâo yàn," with frustration.

She moved the pencil case off her lap and bent down to pick up everything that had fallen onto the floor.

"Tae," someone whispered. Tae looked up to see Becky's smiling face. "Do you need some help?"

Tae quickly nodded and said, "Thank you. That's very nice of you."

The girls gathered all the pens, pencils, and erasers strewn over the floor.

"Tae?" Becky asked. "What did you say before? It sounded neat, even if it was a bit angry."

Tae blushed. She hadn't thought that other people could hear her. But Becky was so nice that Tae said, "My family is from Taiwan, so we speak Mandarin Chinese at home. It's something I say when I'm nervous or when I make trouble."

"Ah! That's really neat!" Becky said.

"It is?"

"Girls," their teacher said, "It's time to take the quiz. The rest of the class is waiting for you to be done cleaning up the mess."

"Sorry, Miss Allen," the girls said together. They scooped up the rest of the pencils and smiled at one another.

Becky whispered, "I want to hear more about Mandarin Chinese language at lunch."

Tae nodded with pride and surprise. She didn't think anyone, even Becky, would want to know more about her home language.

At lunch, Tae walked her tray over to Becky's table, where there were more kids sitting there than normal. When she set her food down she realized that almost the entire group was looking at her.

"Becky told us you can speak two languages," said a kid with freckles and two missing teeth.

Tae looked at Becky, who nodded encouragingly. "I think that it is really cool! Another kid heard me talking to someone about it, and then they called another person over." She shrugged and gave a sheepish grin. "People are really excited to get to know you."

Tae blinked. She was surprised that many kids wanted to know more about her first language. Looking over the sea of faces, she realized that she hadn't spoken to most of them before. Embarrassment started to creep through her chest, and she blushed.

Becky put a comforting hand on Tae's arm. "You don't have to if you don't want to. But I think it's really special."

Tae bit her lip then she smiled. "Okay," she said shyly. "What would you like to know?"

"What is your sandwich called?" Becky asked and pointed to Tae's lunch.

"Sān míng zhì," Tae said.

"Cool!" one boy said. He sat next to Tae with a *thump* and rested his head on his hand. "Can you tell me what 'hair' is in Chinese?"

"Yes, it's tó fâ," Tae said.

"How did you learn to speak two languages?" a little girl with blond pigtails asked.

"My family came here when I was a baby. They speak Mandarin Chinese, but they also helped me learn English for school. My whole family can speak two languages."

"Woah!" said another student. "I want to learn two languages too!"

"I wonder how many languages there are in the world?" another kid Tae had never spoken to said with awe.

Tae thought it was a really good question. She had never thought of it before. But, she looked at Becky, who had a large grin on her face. Had she always known that Tae was a little unhappy? Now that her native language wasn't a secret anymore, her heart felt much lighter.

For the rest of lunch, Tae answered other questions like what "comb," "candy," "bus," and more were—"shū zî," "táng guǒ," "gōng chē." They asked her if she had a different alphabet to learn, to which she said, "Yes, we call it Pinyin. It has a lot of symbols and pictures, like the letters we use in English."

By lunch, Tae felt very comfortable talking about the Chinese part of her life. She was grateful that Becky was her friend.

Tae went over to Becky and threw her arms around Becky's neck. She said, "Xiè xiè!"

Becky laughed and asked, "What does that mean?"

"It means 'Thank you!'" Tae said, laughing, "I think you're my best friend."

"Me too! Can you teach me more Chinese sometime? Can we play together at your house soon?"

Tae nodded and was excited for her family to meet her new friend. She was touched that Becky cared enough to learn more about her. Now she knew that many people liked her for who she was, which meant every part of her.

This idea made her very happy.

She couldn't wait to go home and tell her family how great it was to speak two languages.

Which is exactly what she did.

~ ~ ~

Be comfortable with who you are, learn how to be yourself and to love all of yourself. Try to see past what you think people will expect from you, and you might just be surprised to find out you were wrong about what you thought of them. When you share all of yourself with the people around you, you can help others to grow, love, and learn about new things.

Charlie Bakes Her Dreams

Is there something you dream of doing but think you can't because you're too young, old, not strong enough, or something else? Have you ever thought that maybe, just maybe, you could join something if you were bigger, faster, taller, etc.?

Do you know that it is only these thoughts that hold you back?

If you tell yourself that you're not "something" enough, you might start to believe it. However, if you talk to the voice within that says you're not enough and instead say, "yes, I am," amazing things can happen.

When you say "I can," rather than "I can't," you'll discover that you are big, strong, tall, fast, young, or old enough. Remember that any thoughts or fears you have are small compared to the actions you take. Be afraid, but do something anyway. Hear the thoughts of doubt, but understand you can overcome them.

Listen to your heart and your gut, and follow your passions. You can do anything if you believe in yourself. What is a dream you'd like to accomplish?

Charlie is a girl who loves baking and baking competitions. One day she dreams about joining a baking competition on television but, until then, she keeps practicing. Do you think her dream will become reality?

~ ~ ~

Charlie scrunched her nose up and bit her lip.

She squinted, backed up, and turned her head to the left. Then, she cocked her head to the right.

She took a step forward and smoothed out one side of the cake's pink icing that was a little bit higher than the other. When she removed the metal spatula, she nodded with satisfaction.

A grin spread across her face and pride bloomed in her chest. She looked up at her mom and said, "This is my best cake yet."

Charlie's mom smiled back and said, "It is beautiful. I cannot wait to taste it. What flavor is it?"

"Strawberry with pistachio crunch," Charlie proudly announced.

"Wow, that sounds incredible. I've never thought of combining those two flavors before. You have a very creative baking mind."

Charlie beamed at her mom's compliment. She loved baking and coming up with new flavors, desserts, and recipes. Charlie couldn't wait until she was old enough to try out for the baking competitions on television. The kids on TV were always getting to bake the most amazing things, and Charlie followed each assignment they had. It was her dream to compete in a baking contest.

Sadly, Charlie wasn't old enough to try out for TV baking shows. But she loved baking so much that she kept making sweets for her mom and her family to eat after dinner almost every night of the week.

Charlie started cleaning up her baking equipment when her brother, Peter, ran into the house. He was waving around a green flier and panting heavily. Peter was a few years older than Charlie and a very good older brother. They looked a little bit alike, too. Only Charlie's hair was straight, and Peter's hair was curly. Both had the same light brown hair as their mom and bright blue eyes.

Peter's eyes sparkled as he caught his breath and shoved the flier into Charlie's hands. "Look!" Peter said with excitement. "You can try out for the town's baking competition! It's not on TV, but it's a great place to start!"

Charlie looked at her brother with curiosity, trying to absorb what he was saying. She didn't think she had heard him right and gave him an uncertain look. But then she turned her attention to what the flier said.

CALLING ALL KID BAKERS!!! WE WANT YOU TO BAKE IN OUR COMPETITION. THIS SATURDAY AT 1:00 P.M. GRAND PRIZE FOR WHOEVER WINS ALL THREE ROUNDS: A YEAR'S SUPPLY OF BAKING INGREDIENTS FROM YOUR LOCAL GROCERY STORE.

"Three rounds and a year's supply of baking ingredients!" Charlie shouted. "Think of everything I could bake with that much!" She started jumping around at the thought. "Thank you, Peter! You're the best!" Peter picked up on his sister's excitement, and they started jumping around together.

He laughed. "Your baking is amazing! You're going to win!"

"Alright, everyone. This news is very exciting, but we don't need to shout. Let's turn our excited voices down to a five and you guys can keep jumping around in the play area." Charlie's mom always let her kids feel what they needed, but she sent them to the play area to feel it. And Charlie's mom didn't like shouting in the house.

Charlie and Peter ran into the play area and danced for a few more minutes. Then, Peter asked, "So, are you going to apply tomorrow?"

Charlie looked at the flier again and read what she could on it. "I have to fill out an aaah-p-p-plic-catio-n," she sounded it out. She was still learning to read. Baking also helped her learn about reading because she had to know what ingredients to put into a dessert. However, she was still learning many other words that weren't in recipes.

"Application," Peter said, helping her out. "It means you will have to apply to be in the competition. Usually an application has your name, age, experience level, and other stuff. Mom can help you out with applying." Peter pointed to the flier. "Look, the application forms can be picked up at the library. I bet Mom will take you there tomorrow. Complete it and turn it in, and you'll be ready to bake!"

Peter started dancing around again, but Charlie wasn't as excited. She didn't know how to write very well.

If her mom had to fill out the application, did that mean she shouldn't enter the contest? Charlie let out a long breath and looked at the flier again. Peter stopped jumping and asked, "Why do you look worried?"

"What if I'm too young?" She cried.

20

"That's silly! You're not. You make amazing desserts. You'll be better than everyone else who enters," Peter said confidently.

Charlie smiled at her brother. She loved his support, but it still didn't make the nervous butterflies in her stomach go away.

When Charlie and her mom were filling out the application the next day, Charlie looked at her mom and cautiously asked, "Do you think I'm old enough to do this?"

Charlie's mom placed an arm around her shoulders. "Yes, I think you are very capable of competing. You've been baking since you were two years old. You don't have to be older to compete when you know as much as you know. Age sometimes doesn't matter."

Charlie nodded thoughtfully. What her mom and brother said was very helpful. She decided that she could at least try.

The day of the contest came quickly. Charlie didn't know what she was supposed to bake for the second round because it was a mystery round. But she had gotten to practice for her first and third rounds. She was still nervous. Sometimes, when she baked, the dessert turned out really well but when she got nervous she worried she might miss something important.

Her mom told her, "It's okay to be scared. All you're doing here is practicing. You're practicing for the next competition. No matter what, there will always be another competition to enter. Each time you participate in one, you are learning something. That is what you get to take away. Whether you win or lose, you'll gain some amazing experiences and learn incredible new things. "

Charlie smiled at her mom. She understood. As she entered the tent, Charlie continued to inhale and exhale slowly. This way of slow breathing helped keep her calm, even when her nerves bounced around inside her chest like jumping beans.

Charlie quickly found her place in the tent and put her apron on without needing to be told.

She looked around the large group of people and realized, *This is what it must be like with everyone watching you on TV too.* The thought made her feel even more nervous. Charlie inhaled deeply again and breathed out.

A man in a fancy suit with stripes on his grey jacket and a yellow bowtie stepped up. He said, "All right, kids! Are you ready?"

The kids shouted and cheered, "Yes!"

"Time to get baking!" the announcer said.

Charlie grabbed her baking utensils and ingredients and started making the cupcakes as she had practiced. These cupcakes were chocolate with raspberry filling and raspberry cream cheese icing.

She measured and scooped, and leveled ingredients off. She poured, mixed, and stirred until the mix was a smooth dark brown color. Charlie put a specific amount of mixture in each cupcake cup, and she put the tin into the oven. As she waited for the cupcakes to bake, she cleaned up and realized she wasn't nervous anymore.

Going through the motions of baking helped calm Charlie in a way she didn't think it would. When she figured that out, she started to understand that she did belong in the competition, even if she was the youngest one there.

Charlie did well in the first round and even better in the surprise second round—which had the contestants make a dessert they had never heard of before, a tres leches cake! In the third round, they baked a cake with four layers.

Charlie stood back and looked at her four-layer cake. She had iced it with a new kind of decoration and a unique flavor she hadn't tried before—mint—and, while she was nervous about the taste, she knew that the cake had turned out great. Charlie was very proud of her decorations, she made tiny, colorful balloons from icing, and even made her own sprinkles. She was very happy that Peter had brought the flier home.

When the judges came to try her cake, they smiled at her and gave her a wink.

Then, as the kids stood around holding each other's hands to find out who placed third, second, and first, Charlie's nerves picked up again. She closed her eyes and kept breathing like her mom had taught her. She heard the name "Marion" get called for third place.

"Brian," was called for a second. Charlie began to feel very nervous, she had hoped that she might win second or third place at least, but she didn't think she stood a chance of winning first place. Not when there were lots of older kids there. But then, the judges called out the first-place winner...

"Charlie!"

Charlie opened her eyes and beamed. She couldn't believe that she had won the whole competition! She looked over to her mom and brother and smiled even wider. "I just won a year's worth of baking ingredients!" she yelled over the balloons and cheered. That would help Charlie prepare for many more baking competitions, and with each baking competition she would become a better baker—she couldn't wait to learn more.

~ ~ ~

Follow your passions and dreams—don't wait for something big to happen to you, especially when you have a dream. You have to go after it and work hard to get it. Hard work can make your dreams a reality. You never know what you can achieve if you don't try. Remember to stay kind and caring in the process and keep learning. If you don't succeed straight away, look at it as an opportunity to continue growing and improving.

Martina Learns Lessons and Loves Them

How do you feel when you make a mistake? Does it feel good or bad? Do you say unkind things to yourself when it happens?

Mistakes come in all shapes, sizes, and events. And, to tell you a secret, mistakes are actually amazing! We can never do anything perfectly every time we do it. There are always moments when you can learn, grow, and become better at something—even if it is just putting on your socks.

Mistakes make living a great life possible! Without mistakes, we wouldn't learn anything new.

So, the next time you make a mistake, tell yourself, "Good job! I've just learned a lesson." And tell those unkind thoughts or feelings of embarrassment, anger, or shame to leave you alone.

Martina is a girl who hates making mistakes, but one day she does. How do you think she handled it? What do you do when you make a mistake?

~ ~ ~

Martina opened her eyes and looked out the window.

Crisp colorful leaves were falling, and Martina smiled. The chill in the air meant that the season had changed, and it was right on schedule, which was how she liked things. Although her alarm hadn't gone off, she knew it was about to. Martina always does everything exactly how she is supposed to, and she has gotten into a habit of sticking to a routine.

Just as the alarm beeped for her to get out of bed, Martina sat up and pressed the button for her alarm to stop.

Quiet settled over her bedroom again.

Her legs swung back and forth as she took a deep breath in and slowly released the air out again.

Martina stretched her arms above her head, which gave her a good pulling sensation on all her muscles. It was the perfect way to start her day.

Once she finished her stretch, she made her bed and was sure to iron out any wrinkles in the covers with her hand.

She fluffed her pillows.

She placed her stuffed animals in their positions.

She changed her clothes and folded her pajamas, then placed them into her hamper of dirty clothes.

Martina made her way to school that day. She smiled to herself because it was another perfect morning with no mistakes.

Martina didn't know yet that some mistakes were going to find her anyway.

At the end of the school day, Martina was gathering up her papers, cleaning her desk, and placing things in her book bag, getting ready to go home.

Her teacher looked out to the class and said, "Oh, I'm sorry guys. I forgot to tell you that your project is due by the end of the day on Friday."

Panic pricked at Martina's fingers. Usually, she would add the change to her planner, but she had already put her planner in her book bag to leave for home. If she didn't put in the new deadline, she might forget; if she forgot the deadline change, that wouldn't be perfect. She couldn't let that happen.

She quickly unzipped her book bag, pulled out her planner, and started to write about the new project deadline.

Halfway through, she heard the announcer say, "Bus 17—it's time for you to load up."

"Oh no!" Martina said. "That's my bus." She couldn't miss getting a ride home. Both her parents worked, and she didn't want anyone to have to come to pick her up. That wouldn't be good at all.

Martina shot up from her seat, grabbed her planner with one hand and her book bag with another, and hustled out of the class as quickly as she could without running (because running was against the rules).

She quickly slid into her seat just as the bus took off and sighed in relief that she had made it without being fully prepared. She made a mental note not to let that kind of close call happen again—she didn't like feeling that nervous.

As the bus took off, Martina pulled her backpack closer to her. She started looking through everything to double-check and make sure she had what she needed.

Her homework for the night was missing.

Martina shook her head and huffed out.

"Of course it isn't," she said to herself. She had never forgotten her homework. She couldn't have forgotten now.

But, as she dug through the papers, planner, and folders, Martina realized that nothing she was supposed to do for the night was in her backpack.

"Oh no," she wailed. "The teacher made me forget my homework because she distracted me!" Anger and irritation burned within Martina. Her cheeks heated up, and her fists clenched. She couldn't believe it.

Martina would never have forgotten her homework if Mrs. Windham hadn't changed the due date.

Martina ran her hand through her hair and scrunched up her face wondering, *What am I going to do?*

When the bus dropped Martina off at home, she stomped up to the house, threw the door open and slammed it shut.

The homework problem had put her in a bad mood, and she wasn't afraid to show her emotions.

"Who is home and stomping around?" Martina heard her dad call down the hallway.

"Me. My teacher made me forget my homework," Martina said angrily.

Martina's dad appeared from around the corner. He looked at his daughter and raised his eyebrows, surprised to see that she was so flustered. "Oh?" he said.

"Yes." Martina threw her backpack down and stomped up to her dad. "She distracted me at the end of class by changing the project deadline. I didn't put my papers in my book bag like always." Martina placed her hands on her hips and stamped her foot.

Martina's dad was a good-humored fellow. Although he knew that his daughter's feelings were important, he also knew her anger was misplaced. "Actually, sweetie, that sounds like you made a mistake."

Shock shot through Martina. "What?" she asked in disbelief.

"Well, it sounds like the teacher was doing her job. What if she hadn't told you about the project deadline? Then, how would you know?" Her dad reasoned.

Martina's arms dropped as she realized her father was right, but instead of feeling relieved, she let the weight of the word "mistake" press on her shoulders. "I made a mistake?" she asked in a small voice.

Martina couldn't remember the last time she made a mistake. As the realization washed over her, worry started to prickle her chest. She looked at her dad, whose features softened, even more when he saw his daughter grow so upset. He stooped down and placed a hand on her shoulder. "Sweetie, why are you upset now?"

Tears built up and burst over her cheeks. She began to sob and stutter, "I-I-I made a mis-s-s-take!"

Martina's dad sighed and sat on the floor. He pulled his daughter into his lap and gave her a hug. As he stroked her hair, he rocked her gently and said, "It's okay. Mistakes are a good thing. They give you the chance to think creatively, solve problems, and learn new things about yourself."

Martina hiccuped.

She rubbed her tears away from her cheek.

She remembered that her dad had said something like that to her before.

"What do you mean?" she sniffled.

"Listen, you are a really good girl and a great daughter. But, you put so much pressure on yourself to be 'perfect' when there is no such thing as perfect. We are all different and unique. You like to keep your bed nice and neat. Your brother clumps everything up on it." Martina laughed at the thought of her brother's room. It was very messy. "But that doesn't mean anything bad about him, does it?"

Martina shook her head. While her brother was a bit messy, he was a nice person who was always kind to everyone. He also got very good grades and was very helpful with the neighbors.

"Perfection doesn't mean that your life will be free from stress. It means that when you keep trying to be perfect, you're missing out on all the moments that you can learn from to know more about who you are and how you handle change or a challenge. Mistakes are amazing."

Martina sniffled one more time. She was beginning to understand what her dad was saying.

He gave her a big hug and said, "Think about how you can fix your problem."

Martina stood up and helped her dad do the same. "Well," she said, "I could tell the teacher that I didn't remember to bring my papers home for homework."

"Yes! That's a great solution to your problem. Do you see how easy it was to problem-solve? If you hadn't forgotten your homework, you wouldn't have gotten to use your brain like that. How does it feel?"

Martina smiled. "Pretty good!'

Later that night, Martina was lying in bed, and she wondered what it would be like to not make her bed in the morning. When she woke up, she tried not to make it like she always did, but she couldn't resist and made it her way. While it was perfect for her, she knew now it might not be perfect for everyone else.

Martina knew that any other mistakes she made would be a great way to learn, grow, and succeed.

And she was happy with that.

~ ~ ~

Learn from your mistakes and negative adversity—when you learn from the mistakes you make, you can grow in ways you could never have imagined. You'll become more amazing than you already are. Look at your mistakes as lessons to be learned, not things that are "wrong" or "bad."

Alice Makes a Splash!

Are there things that you are afraid of? Do you try and tell your fear to go away when it pops up? Or do you let your fear prevent you from doing something because you aren't sure what will happen?

Being cautious is always a good thing, but make sure that you are not letting your fear stop you from trying new activities. Sometimes, a challenge is so big and unique that your fear may tell you that you cannot do what you want to. But, if it is something that will help you grow and no one will get hurt when you do it, you should try anyway.

Even if you are afraid, you need to do it anyway to surprise yourself.

Alice is a girl who loves adventure and is rarely afraid of anything. She never lets her fear win, but when she encounters a new kind of challenge, her fear seems to take control. What do you think happens?

Do you ever feel afraid of things?

What do you do when you are scared?

~ ~ ~

Alice pumped her legs backward and forward to make her swing fly higher. She looked to her left to see how high her friends were. Her hair whipped around her face. Although she couldn't see them, she knew she was swinging higher and faster than them. She had always loved gliding through the air quickly on the swing set.

She shook her head back to face forward and closed her eyes as the warm sun warmed her cheeks and face.

"Alice! It's time to go," she heard someone call. Alice opened her eyes and saw her parents waiting for her at the playground's edge. They were going to the lake today and, while Alice was waiting for her parents to pack up, she had seen her friends going to play. She knew that she could get in some play time with them too.

Alice let go of the chains and leaped from the swing, jumping mid-air.

The kids in her group *ooh'd* and *aah'd* as she landed on her feet.

While she knew it wasn't something she could do at every playground, she had practiced it in the neighborhood many times and knew the right height to leap from where she wouldn't get hurt.

Alice was always making sure she was safe first. Even though she liked adventure, her parents always told her that there were right and wrong ways to do some things. And since she didn't want to get hurt, she kept her parents' advice in her mind at all times.

"Bye, guys!" Alice called, running to her parents while she waved goodbye to her friends. She couldn't wait to get to the lake.

Each year, Alice's family took a trip up to the lake. They stayed a few days in the same cabin, and while they were there, they always did many fun things. They climbed rocks, went canoeing, played in the lake, jumped on a water trampoline, and much, much more.

This year, Alice and her family were going somewhere different. Going to a lake they hadn't been to before meant that they would have new adventures and get to do a bunch of new things.

Alice's excitement bubbled over as soon as they got to the camping ground. She looked at all the things there were to do. She saw a huge slide into the lake, a merry-go-round, an outdoor theater with a movie screen, and more. But what caught her interest the most was a line of kids running up to the tallest point over the lake, grabbing a rope, and swinging into the water. Each kid landed with a huge splash. Alice said to herself, "I'm going to make the biggest splash."

Alice bounced on her toes as they unpacked their car and got their cabin ready. The longer she had to wait to jump into the lake, the higher her excitement and motivation went. She kept thinking about all the different flips, flops, jumps, and dives she could do, and in her imagination, each splash was bigger and grander than the next one.

She finally got a chance to get her swimsuit on, and she took her mom by the hand, pulling her along the path toward the hill with the swinging jump.

"Alice, calm down, sweetie." Alice turned to look back at her mom who gave her a kind smile.

She said, "I'm sorry. I've just never seen something like that swing before. I'm going to make the biggest splash!"

Her mom laughed and replied, "That sounds like a great goal. You don't have to pull on my arm, though. Why don't you go stand in line? I'm going to look around and see what else we can do. I'll be back over before you jump, okay?"

Alice nodded and took off, running toward the line before her mom could say anything else.

Standing at the bottom of the hill, she craned her neck up, and up, and up, and she still couldn't see where the line to swing on was. "Woah," she whispered. Alice realized how tall the hill really was. If she couldn't see the top, her splash into the lake would be huge!

Alice waited patiently in line. She looked around, talked to other kids around her, and asked them about the hill swing. All the kids said it was the best thing they'd ever done.

"Amazing!"

"So fun!"

"I splashed down so hard!"

But, as the line began to move and Alice crept up the hill, she looked back down to where the end of the line started. She was already higher up than she had ever been. Even when she was swinging.

Alice swallowed.

She searched the crowd for her mom and dad but couldn't see them in the sea of people.

She swallowed again.

Fear started to poke up its little fingers inside her chest.

She scratched at it and muttered, "Go away, fear. I'm going to do this."

But even as she said it, she wasn't so sure.

She could hear the doubt in her voice and feel her lip tremble.

Although she had never felt fear too much before, Alice knew she was afraid.

Her teeth clenched together, and she wrung her towel between her hands.

Her eyes started to dart around a little more. She really wanted to hug her mom.

The need was so great that she looked back at where she had come from. When she looked forward again, she realized that it was almost her turn to jump and decided that she would just go find her family now instead. Then she could hug her mom, and everything would be better.

She turned to the kid she had spoken to a little while waiting in line and said, "I think I have to go find my mom. Thanks!" Alice waved and ran back down the hill quickly, shortening her steps to make sure that she didn't fall down the steep ground underneath her feet.

As soon as she reached flat land, she saw her parents and flung herself at her mom's waist. Alice hugged her mom tightly. "Alice," her mom gasped. "Alice, what's wrong?"

Alice's mom put her arms around her daughter and hugged her back, "I don't want to go on the swing up there. It is too high." Alice said, burying her head into her mom's shoulder.

"Oh boy," Alice's mom crouched down to Alice's level, and her dad wiped a few tears away from Alice's cheek. "I've never seen you scared before. It must have been really frightening."

Alice nodded.

"What do you think was so scary about it?" Alice's dad asked.

"It's really, really, really, high! Then, you're supposed to jump, and you don't know what the water will feel like, or what it will feel like falling through the air." Alice tried to take a breath but couldn't stop her worried thoughts from tumbling out of her mouth in a rush.

Alice's mom placed her hands on Alice's shoulders. "Ssshhhh, take a big, deep breath," her mom said, and Alice listened, gulping in air. "Now, slowly let the breath out," her mom instructed. Alice blew out, already feeling a bit better. "Okay. You don't have to go up that hill and jump off of it. You know that, right?"

Alice bit her lip and looked up the hill again. She nodded. "I want to, though."

"Well then, you'll have to work past your fear," Alice's mom said.

"You know that when you're afraid of something, it just means that you care about doing what you want to do very much," her dad told her. "We all feel fear when we're trying something new or when what we are doing is something very important. Fear is just an alarm to let you know to be careful. But, sometimes, it gets overwhelming. If you want to jump off that hill, you must accept your fear but jump anyway."

Alice looked back up the hill.

Her chest tightened, thinking about walking back up the hill and jumping off at the top.

But, her sense of adventure, her mind, and her gut were whispering, "Do it. Do it. Do it. Jump!"

She looked at her parents and asked, "Will you come with me?"

Alice's parents looked at each other and smiled, then turned to Alice. "Of course we will, sweetie," her mom promised.

They took her hands and walked her over to the end of the line.

The second time Alice climbed the hill, it didn't seem quite so tall. But, whenever she felt anxious, she squeezed one of her parent's hands. Before she knew it, they were at the top of the hill. This time, it didn't take as long, either.

Alice realized that having her parents there for support was a good thing.

She also realized that, since it was her second time up the hill, things didn't seem quite so scary. Until she reached the tippy top. When they were there, her chest tightened up a little more, but she talked to her fear and asked, "Fear, what are you afraid of?"

Her fear whispered, "Falling."

"We aren't going to fall. We are going to jump!"

When Alice opened her eyes, she realized that her fear wasn't really afraid of anything real because she was going to jump, and she was good at jumping. Alice smiled at her mom and dad and said, "Thank you for coming with me!"

They gave her a hug and saw that she was ready to jump.

Alice took the rope, ran toward the edge, and leapt off with a big yell.

She let go and flew into the water with a huge splash!

When she broke through the top of the water, she saw her parents and the rest of the crowd cheering her on. She really had made the biggest splash!

~ ~ ~

45

When you build your confidence, you can silence your inner critic—understand that many things in the world can be scary. Still, when you give in to fear, you won't be able to live your best life. As long as you are safe, do everything you want to do, no matter what your fear tells you.

Emily Makes a Difference

It doesn't matter how young or old you are. You can still make a difference in someone's life. Sometimes people need help, but they don't know how to ask. Other times, people don't want to ask for help because they are worried they will add a burden to other people's lives. But sometimes, just doing a nice deed for someone can brighten their day.

Whatever your reason for helping another person or animal is, you are carving out a little space in their heart for you and making an impact on their life.

If you want to help someone, the best thing you can do is surprise them with your niceness. When you are kind, you show people that you are thinking of them, which is the best way to make a difference.

Emily sees that her neighbor might need some help, but she worries that she might be too young to be useful. What do you think happens for her to realize she can still find ways to be useful? How would you have helped your neighbor?

~ ~ ~

Confused, Emily scrunched her eyebrows together and erased the number she just wrote.

The math problem she was working on was a real doozy but she was determined to fix it. Not only because it was homework that she had to finish, but also because she loved solving problems.

Emily tapped the pencil eraser on the bottom of her lip as she tried to sort through the numbers in her mind when something outside caught her attention. She looked up and saw that Mrs. Brown, their neighbor, was walking up to her house with crutches.

"Uh-oh," Emily said to herself, "I wonder what happened?" She put her pencil down and went into her dad's office. Her dad worked from home.

Normally, Emily didn't go into the office while he was working. Still, since it was Saturday, she knew that he probably wasn't busy and was most likely just tidying up.

"Dad?" Emily asked.

"Yes?"

"Mrs. Brown is walking on crutches."

"She is?" Her Dad looked up and out the window. "That is terrible. I wonder what happened."

"I think we should go check on her," Emily said.

Her dad smiled and replied, "Sure. Let's go. That is a very kind observation and thought, sweetie."

Emily smiled back at him. She liked to know that her dad thought she was kind. She slipped her hand into his and they walked across the lawn to Mrs. Brown's front porch. Emily rang the doorbell and she swung her dad's arm back and forth while they waited.

"Hello," Mrs. Brown answered a few moments later. "Oh! Emily and Jim, hello. How are you doing?" Mrs. Brown hopped backward on her crutches and opened the screen door further. She sounded surprised.

Emily's dad held the door for Emily and they walked in.

"Would you mind if I went to sit down? This broken leg has made me very tired," Mrs. Brown said, blowing out a long breath.

Emily and her dad shook their heads no and followed Mrs. Brown into the next room. Before they sat down, Emily asked Mrs. Brown, "What happened to your leg? How did you hurt yourself?" Emily sat on the squishy, green, stuffed chair she usually used when she came over, and she watched her dad help Mrs. Brown get seated.

With a groan, Mrs. Brown sat down and said, "I was at work and fell down the stairs. I landed in an awkward position on my leg, breaking it in two places. Luckily for me, it was below my knee, or I would have had a cast up to my hip."

Emily did not think it sounded lucky at all but agreed that having a cast up to her hip would not be good either. "That sounds bad," Emily said.

"It's okay, dear. After just a few weeks of recovery, I'll be as good as new. Probably even better than before."

Emily nodded and smiled. She didn't want to disagree with Mrs. Brown when she had just hurt herself, but she didn't understand how breaking something could make it better. But Emily guessed it wasn't that important because Mrs. Brown kept talking. "I'll have to hire someone to help me around the house for a few weeks until I'm all mended. All of my family lives out of state and cannot fly over here just because I'm a little hurt."

Emily looked at her dad, smiling and nodding along with what Mrs. Brown said. He didn't seem shocked that she didn't have someone to help her, but Emily surely was.

Once they were done visiting Mrs. Brown, Emily and her dad left. As they walked back to their house, Emily said, "That's really sad she doesn't have any family members close to her that can help."

"It is," her dad agreed.

"How do you think we can help her out?" Emily bit her lip, she was unsure of what she could do to help out her neighbor, but she definitely wanted to help Mrs. Brown out.

"You know, that is a really sweet offer. I'm not sure. Why don't we think about it, and we can talk about it over dinner tonight? You will have to finish up your homework, right?" her dad asked.

Emily nodded distractedly, the problem-solving cogs in her mind already whirling away.

At dinner, Emily announced to her dad, "I think we can help Mrs. Brown by doing yard work."

"Yard work? Can you explain a bit more what you're thinking?"

"She probably has to rest a lot, right? You always say I need rest when I'm sick or hurt," Emily said thoughtfully.

"This is true," her dad agreed.

Emily Makes a Difference

"So, instead of helping her INSIDE, we can help her OUTSIDE. We already work outside our house so we can use our equipment and help her. That way, we won't have to interrupt her rest," Emily said getting excited.

"Emily, that is a great idea. What kind of yard work do you think we should do?"

Emily tapped her bottom lip with her finger while she thought. "You can mow the lawn, right?" Emily said.

"Yes, I can mow her yard. I don't think you're old enough to mess around with a lawn mower."

"Okay. What else does her yard need?" Emily asked.

Emily's dad looked outside the window and said, "Well, it looks like the leaves are falling, and her flower beds need to be weeded. You can definitely do both of those things."

"I've never done anything with leaves before, Dad," Emily said, worried.

Her dad knelt and kissed her forehead. "Don't worry, I can show you. We can do that together. Let's go over it tomorrow morning and start. We can do the leaves together, then you can weed while I mow."

"Sounds good," Emily happily agreed.

"Your idea is also good. It is very thoughtful and special for you to think of Mrs. Brown when she isn't feeling well. Thanks for being such a good kid, Emily."

Emily beamed. She was proud that her dad thought she was a good kid.

The next morning, Emily and her dad raked up the leaves. Emily's dad showed her how to use a rake to make leaf piles. Then, they would pick up the leaves and put them into large paper bags so the garbage people could come to pick them up.

Mrs. Brown's front yard had four large oak trees, and Emily thought they would never finish raking. One of the more frustrating things for Emily was that the leaves kept falling.

Emily's dad laughed. "We will probably have to clean up the leaves again, but for now, let's get as much as we can done. Plus, leaves are great for jumping in." Emily tilted her head to the side and asked, "What do you mean?"

"Watch!" Emily's dad said. He showed her how to make huge piles and said, "Run and jump in!"

When Emily did, she slid under the leaves like she was sliding into home plate during baseball. The leaves rustled and rained down upon her. She sat up quickly and laughed. "That was fun!"

When she finished raking the leaves with her dad, he went to get the lawn mower, and she grabbed a garbage bag. Emily walked over to the flower beds and started picking out all the long green, brown, and other colors of weeds that she knew did not belong in Mrs. Brown's flower bed.

After the rest of the yard work was done, Emily and her dad put the bags of leaves and weeds in the front of Mrs. Brown's driveway for when the garbage people came to pick up the trash. When Emily turned around, she saw Mrs. Brown standing with her crutches on her front porch. She had a look of shock and happiness on her face.

Emily and her dad went up to Mrs. Brown to say hi.

"Oh, my dears. The yard looks beautiful. Thank you so much for your help!" Mrs. Brown looked around her clean yard and tears glistened in her eyes. She was very surprised and touched at her neighbor's kindness.

Emily hugged Mrs. Brown and said, "We just wanted to make you feel better somehow."

"This does make me feel better! How thoughtful and kind."

A few weeks later, Emily heard a knock on the door.

She went to open it and found Mrs. Brown with no crutches. She held a golden brown pie in her hands. "It's an apple pie because I know it's your favorite."

"Wow! Thank you!" Emily gasped delightedly.

"Thank you too! I feel amazing now, and I'm better than ever." Mrs. Brown stated proudly.

Mrs. Brown came into Emily's house, and the three of them each had a big piece of pie with a scoop of vanilla ice cream.

And it was delicious.

~ ~ ~

No one is too young or insignificant to make a difference—when you think of an idea, don't be afraid to tell people about it. All the ideas you have are important and needed in the world. Even when you think they are not. You bring a special gift into the world, and only you can share it. Being kind and helping others can not only make them feel amazing but can make you feel great too.

Candice is Kind

There are a lot of times when you may feel grumpy, angry, annoyed, or some other type of negative emotion. But don't push these feelings away. They are part of who you are and are important to have. When you feel down or upset, it's a good time to remember to love yourself or to seek comfort from someone who loves you.

These emotions let you know when you need a little extra kindness. When you are kind to yourself in these moments, you can learn to be kind to others who need love and compassion in grumpy times.

Candice is a girl who has one of those cranky times. Luckily, she has a good friend to help her through it. How do you think her friend's kindness helps Candice?

When you are in a grumpy mood, what do you do to cheer yourself up? Do you do anything that makes you feel better? Who are the people in your life that can help shake you out of your bad mood?

~ ~ ~

Candice rolled over.

She did not want to wake up.

Her bed was comfortable and warm.

She shifted in bed.

She didn't sleep well the night before, and she was tired.

She refused to get up. She won't go to school today. She just wanted to sleep. She didn't care what her mom said. . .

"Candice, it's time to wake up," her mom called.

Candice opened one eye to look at her mom and threw an arm over her face to cover her eyes. "No," Candice grumbled.

"Candice. It's time to wake up. We go through this every morning. Now, you must get up," her mom persisted.

"I don't want to go to school," Candice moaned.

"I know, sweetie. But you have to. It's part of life," Candice's mom said kindly.

Candice grumbled. She rolled over and decided that if she had to get up, at least she could be grumpy about it.

As Candice pulled on her shirt, she realized how itchy the shirt's tag was on her back. She struggled to reach it and tried to tuck it into a different position so it stopped scratching, but it didn't help. So, she kept twitching uncomfortably as she got ready.

The tag scratching at her skin made her a little more grumpy.

Candice moved to put her socks on, but one sock kept slumping. It seemed as though it was stretched out a little too much. Just enough for her to realize that her socks didn't match. She decided to leave it there. If her mom was going to make her go to school, then Candice would wear the slumpy sock because her mom was the one who made her get up.

Candice stomped down the stairs and grunted at her mom.

Her mom placed a plate of breakfast food on the table in front of her. Candice crossed her arms, pouting. She shook her leg to make sure the sock slumped even more. She shifted in her seat because her tag was still bothering her.

"Candice, eat some breakfast. It will help you feel better," her mom sighed.

"No."

Her mom sighed and said, "Well, if you choose to be grumpy, the only person you truly hurt is yourself."

Candice scrunched her nose and held her arms tighter across her chest. She knew what her mom was saying was true, but she could not seem to get out of her bad mood now.

Candice had to wait in line to go to the bathroom during school. She groaned loudly, stamping her feet.

A girl in front of her turned around and gave Candice an irritated look.

Candice matched her look and whined, "This line is sooooo long. I have to go to the bathroom."

The girl in front of her shrugged, rolled her eyes, and turned back to face the front.

Candice felt a tap on her shoulder and whipped her head around to see her friend Sandy.

Sandy's warm smile took Candice by surprise. "Hi," Sandy said. "It looks like you need a hug."

"What?" Candice responded.

"You need a hug. Can I give you one?"

Candice raised her eyebrows at Sandy, she was unsure why Sandy thought she needed a hug. Candice replied, "Sure." But secretly she wondered how a hug could possibly help her.

Sandy hugged Candice. She said, "I know sometimes things in life are hard, but I love you."

The warmth of Sandy's hug and her kind words touched Candice's heart. And Candice realized she felt better.

When she pulled out of the hug, she said, "Thank you. I love you too! That really helped me."

Sandy smiled. "Sometimes, when we are our most grumpy, that is when we need the most love." She laughed. "At least, that is what my mom says."

Candice smiled. It felt good to smile. She really did feel better. When she turned around in the line, she realized it was her turn to go to the bathroom.

Later that day, Candice went to sit next to her friends at lunch. Her bad mood had dissolved, and she had smiled all day since Sandy had hugged her. Sandy's words also affected Candice, and she wanted to make sure that she passed along that message to other people who may need some help with being less grumpy or angry.

Candice noticed AJ was sitting a little bit away, separated from the rest of her friend group. Normally, AJ laughed loudly and made a spectacle of himself. Today, he was slumped over and looked angry as he grumbled at his french fries.

Candice placed her tray down next to AJ and sat next to him. She asked, "Is everything okay?"

AJ said, "No." He did not look her way, blink his eyes, or do anything but stare at the wall.

"Do you want to talk about it?" Candice asked.

"No." AJ mumbled.

"Okay. I'll just sit here with you," Candice said. She didn't want to push anyone into doing anything they weren't comfortable with, especially when they weren't in a good mood. Candice didn't like it when someone tried to push her into those things. So, she wouldn't do it to anyone else.

After they ate in silence, AJ got up to throw away his trash. But he didn't come back. Candice didn't think it was good for him to be alone, so she got up to go look for him. After she cleared away her own food, she saw that he had gone to sit at a table by himself again.

She walked over and sat next to him, but not too close. While she didn't say anything, he looked over at her and asked, "What are you doing?"

"I wanted to let you know that you weren't alone, even when you feel that way."

AJ crossed his arms over his chest and his legs at the ankles. "I don't want you to be around me."

"I know." Candice responded.

"Then why are you?" AJ asked grumpily.

"Because, sometimes, when we are our moodiest, we need the most love."

"That's the dumbest thing I ever heard! I want you to leave me alone!" AJ yelled.

Candice smiled and said, "Okay, but I'm here if you want to talk. I'll just be down at the end of the table reading."

AJ groaned and slumped back against the wall.

Candice moved down to the edge of the lunch table, pulled out a book, and started to read. She kept her promise and was there with AJ until it was time to go back to class.

On her way to the bus, Candice saw AJ again. He didn't look like he was in a happy mood, but it did look like his mood had lifted a little. She walked over to him and said, "Can I give you a hug?"

AJ blinked. "Um. Sure."

Candice wrapped her arms around his neck and hugged him. She said, "I hope you have a better day after school and a better day tomorrow too."

Then, she turned around and got onto her bus.

The next morning, AJ came up to Candice, who was talking and laughing with Sandy. He said, "H-hello, Candice?"

Candice and Sandy turned to look at AJ.

Candice gave AJ a big smile and said, "Hi! How are you feeling today?"

"Much better, thank you!" AJ smiled. His goofy grin showed a few gaps in his teeth from where they were still growing.

"That's great!" Candice exclaimed.

"Yes, I wanted to apologize for being cranky with you yesterday. I'm sorry about what I said." AJ said bashfully.

"That's okay. Sandy is the one who told me that people who are angry or grumpy need the most kindness." Candice explained.

"Eh, I didn't mean what I said. I was just in a really bad mood. But you being a good friend and not leaving me alone, even when I yelled at you, was very nice. I also didn't know that I needed a hug. It really helped!" A J said.

Candice and Sandy smiled at him.

"Trust me, I totally understand!" Candice laughed at how grumpy she was the day before. "I'm really glad I could help you," she said. Then she turned to Sandy. "Without your hug, I wouldn't have been able to help AJ. So, thank you too."

Sandy threw one arm around AJ and one around Candice and said, "You're welcome! Thank you, too, for being such good friends."

~ ~ ~

When you use kindness and empathy, you can learn how to be kind to others because you'll never know when you need help. Putting others' needs before your own allows you to think outside of yourself and keeps your heart open to kindness. People who love us and who we love will bring us joy, compassion, and kindness. These gifts will help you out in incredible ways and give you the inspiration to accomplish amazing things.

Julie and Ashley Work Together

Working together as a team can sometimes be difficult, especially when you have different ideas on how to do things. But each group member can bring amazing ideas to the table. Remember that everyone's voice is equally important and that no thought is small. Consider everything to see all angles and views. Even if you don't end up using someone else's ideas or even if your idea doesn't get used, you and your team can be sure you've included everyone.

This next story has two girls who aren't friends but need to work together. Ashley and Julie are away at camp and are placed in a group where they have to work together so their troop gets to have their talent show. What do you think happens when they start to misunderstand each other? Do you think they can learn to communicate before the show takes place?

How would you figure out to work with someone who communicates differently?

~ ~ ~

"For the Wilderness Group Talent Show, the group is Ashley, Julie, Meredith, and Sylvia. Your team is responsible for making sure that the talent show stage is built by the end of the week," the head troop master announced.

Ashley shook her head. She didn't believe it. How were they supposed to build an entire stage by the end of the week? She knew it must be possible. Otherwise, the head troop master would not have assigned it to them, but it seemed like a huge project for only four people.

She started to break down the tasks in her mind when the morning gathering ended with the official blow of a horn. Ashley jumped at the sound, looked around, and decided to find the head troop master to see what their next steps were.

Julie had a different idea.

She wanted to gather up the members of the stage-building team so they could get a plan in action. Julie understood the big task ahead of them. She knew they had to start planning immediately so everything could go as smoothly as possible.

Julie found Meredith and Sylvia quickly, but their team had trouble finding Ashley until Julie saw her talking to the headmaster.

Julie crossed her arms over her chest and raised an eyebrow, thinking, *Why would she be talking to the headmaster without us*? Julie looked at her other two team members, chatting excitedly about what they would do for the talent show, and said to them, "I see Ashley. Let's go get her."

The girls wound their way through the other teams clumped together. They were all talking about their team assignments. Julie tried not to feel annoyed that they weren't already planning like the rest. She knew it was probably the biggest part of the week and that Ashley didn't think to find her team first irked Julie.

When they arrived at where the headmaster was standing, Julie heard Ashley say, "Thank you, head troop master! That is very helpful!"

Ashley turned around and beamed when she saw her group. She ran up to them and said, "Head Troopmaster Florence gave me the instructions for the stage and she pointed out all the supplies, tools, and placing of the stage. I think we should go to the area and then we can check things out."

Julie crossed her arms tighter across her chest and gave Ashley a dirty look. "You could ask us what our thoughts are first," she snapped.

Ashley blanched. She hadn't expected anger from her team member. "Um. Yes. What would you like to do?"

Julie relaxed and said, "We can go to the area where the stage is supposed to be put up."

Ashley scrunched her face at Julie and said, "If that was your answer, why would you snap at me?" She couldn't understand why Julie would be annoyed when she'd suggested what she had wanted to do anyway.

Julie shrugged. "I just don't think you were thinking about the rest of us, that's all."

"Maybe. Maybe not. But I was thinking about how we could get the stage built," Ashley said.

"Yes, but if you found us, we could have made a plan," Julie snipped.

"Well, this isn't going to work," Ashley said exasperatedly. She turned and stormed off in the direction of the troop master.

Julie was fast on her heels. She grabbed Ashley's arm and asked, "What are you doing?"

"I don't want to work with you. You jumped on me as soon as you saw me. I don't think that's very good teamwork." Ashley said pulling away from Julie.

"Well, I don't want to work with you either. You thought of yourself before you thought of your team and I don't think that is very good team work." Julie snapped.

Both girls stomped toward their group leader, Miss Lilac, and bombarded her with requests, suggestions, and frustrations. Neither girl waited for the other to finish speaking. Their actions shocked Miss Lilac and she took a step back.

She held up her hands and said, "Woah. Girls. Stop."

Both girls bit their lips. They were breathing heavily.

"Where are your other group members?"

Julie flinched. She had forgotten about them. She sheepishly turned to see both Meredith and Sylvia standing behind them with worried looks in their eyes. The whole point of Julie fighting with Ashley was so they could be a team, and the moment Julie got annoyed she forgot about what she was fighting for. That didn't make Julie feel very good.

Ashley looked over to her teammates and realized there was a different way she could have handled things from the look on their faces.

"I want to do a different project," Ashley said. "Julie just jumped on me and didn't say thank you for the work I already did. I don't think she and I will work well together. We've already forgotten about our other team members." Ashley waved her hands to Meredith and Sylvia standing awkwardly at the side.

"I don't want to work with Ashley," Julie said. "She didn't even think to find us first." Her irritation had deflated a little because she realized she hadn't been a good team member either when she forgot about her other teammates. Still, she dug her heels in because she didn't think that Ashley had done anything right, and Julie didn't want to admit that she could have done things a little differently.

Miss Lilac looked at the four girls and said, "Meredith and Sylvia, what do you think?"

Meredith shrugged, "I don't think either of them did very well. I was just excited to do something for the talent show. It's my favorite part of camp."

Sylvia looked at her feet. "I'm not comfortable with how they are yelling at each other."

Miss Lilac nodded and said, "Okay, girls, why don't you form your own team? You can come up with the decorations for the stage and the talent show area. I'll show you where some supplies are in a few moments. Please let me speak with Ashley and Julie."

Sylvia and Meredith nodded, looking relieved, and went off holding hands, giggling, and chatting. Julie grimaced at how much happier they looked. She turned to Miss Lilac. "Can I go work with them?"

"No."

Julie's shoulders slumped.

Miss Lilac stepped back. She looked Ashley and Julie over and tapped on her chin for a few moments. "I think you girls need to figure out how to work together. You'll both build the stage."

"What?! We just lost two people," Ashley moaned.

"Yes, you did. It happened because neither of you thought about what was best for the team. You made them feel uncomfortable. Now you have to figure out how to do all the work for four people with only two. Meet the deadline and work together. If you don't complete the stage by the end of the week, you will both let the entire camp down. Let me know if you need anything, girls. Bye!" Miss Lilac walked away without letting either girl say anything else.

They stood with their mouths agape for a few moments.

"Well, that wasn't good," Julie muttered, returning to herself first.

"No. It wasn't." Ashley agreed.

"Well, at least we can agree on one thing," Julie laughed.

Ashley looked at her and said, "I'm not sure this will work."

"Me either. But we have to try."

Ashley shrugged and blew out a long breath. "Well, let's go over to the stage area and make a plan."

The girls looked through all the supplies and made a note on all the items to make sure that they had everything. Julie said, "I think I can start the frame if you want to work on the base. That way, we are getting things done without getting in each other's way."

"Good idea," Ashley said, and she went over to the wood and tools. "I'm going to set up shop over there," she pointed to an area closer to the woods so she could be farther away from Julie.

"Okay, let me know when you need help carrying it over to the stage area."

"I will."

The girls separated and started on their parts.

Ashley hammered corners.

Julie drilled planks.

Ashley sanded wood.

Julie kept going.

"Oh no!" Ashley heard Julie call. Ashley put her hammer down and ran over to where Julie was sitting.

"What's wrong?" Ashley asked.

"I did this one instruction backward, and now the base will not work." Julie sat down defeatedly.

"It's okay, look! We can flip the whole part over, and nothing will be messed up," Ashley reassured her. Julie popped her head up and looked at what Ashley said.

"Wow. That's a good idea!" Julie said gratefully.

"Thanks!"

After that moment, Ashley and Julie became fast friends. They realized how hard work and communication go hand-in-hand. They also found out that they had a lot in common. So much so that they performed on the stage they built in the talent show together.

They got a standing ovation.

~ ~ ~

You don't have to do it all alone—Each person in the world may have similar thoughts and ideas, but no one is just like you. Each of us is unique and can bring good ideas to the table when working as a team. Sometimes others will have different ways they want to do something, remember that every person's ideas are important, finding a way to work together, and listening to all opinions as much as possible will give you a wonderful experience and new lessons to learn.

Liza Wins the Cup

Have you ever seen someone doing something and wondered how they do it so well? Have you ever thought about asking them? Did you know that you can? When other people do something well, it is because they practice at it. They've taken bumps and bruises; they've fallen and gotten back up. They've gotten frustrated, confused, and even thought about quitting.

But they didn't.

And you shouldn't either.

When you discover something that you are interested in, you should try it out. See if you like it. If you do enjoy it and want to get better, understand that you will have some hard times along the way. These are the moments where you grow and learn, even if they may feel bad. The times when you grow lead you to another level on your journey of doing your best, and that is never a bad thing.

Liza is the girl in our next story, she wants to win the riding cup for horse tricks but she worries that she can't do the same tricks older riders do. What do you think happens as she finds the courage to try them?

Have you ever wanted to try something but were afraid to? How did you end up doing it?

~ ~ ~

"Come on, Candy. We're going to make that next jump," Liza whispered to her horse as they waited for their turn.

The jump was higher than any Candy and Liza had jumped before, but that didn't scare Liza.

She knew they could do it because her horse was the best jumper in the county. Candy was also the most beautiful horse—she had a chestnut-colored coat and a black shining mane. Her eyes were large and the color of coal. Her eyelashes were long, thick, and added kindness to Candy's eyes.

Candy also had tan markings along her flank, which made her look like she was wearing pants.

Liza trotted up to the starting point and nudged Candy forward when it was her turn. Liza coaxed Candy to go faster with a "Hee-yah!" They sped up.

She needed more speed, so she squeezed her horse's sides with her heels, and Candy got to the top place she needed to be. With another yell of "Up!" Liza moved her body into the right position to urge Candy to jump.

They soared through the air, with only Candy's back hoof tagging the bar. It bounced a little with a slight *clunk* and as Candy landed with all four hooves on the ground, the bar settled back into its place.

A smile burst over Liza's face. She hugged Candy and said, "Great job, girl!" The horse twitched her ears and nickered at Liza.

Liza could tell by the sound of Candy's nicker that she was pleased with herself too.

After they jumped a few more times, Candy and Liza were tired. Liza led her horse back to the stable and took time to wash Candy down, brush her, and give her some special treats for how well she did.

When it was time to leave, Liza pet Candy good-bye, covered her up with a warm blanket in her stall and left the stable for the day.

Liza turned her head to see the bulletin board for the stables. All the information, like contests and announcements, was on the bulletin board. A yellow flier flicked in the breeze. Liza stepped up to it because it hadn't been there at the beginning of her practice.

BEST TRICK COMPETITION!

SILVER CUP PRIZE!

WHAT: Compete against students your age to win the silver cup of your age bracket.

WHEN: Two weeks from now.

"Two weeks is not a lot of time," Liza mumbled.

But she really wanted to be in the competition. She would have to think about some new tricks to do because everyone who was her age had learned the same tricks. Liza walked out of the stables, deep in thought.

The next morning, she came back and watched the older kids practice. Liza realized if she wanted to stand out, she would have to try something a little more challenging.

Although some of the tricks did seem to be too complicated to learn in two weeks, Liza did see one girl do a fun spin, then hop with her horse. That could be im-pressive if Liza did it at the end of a jump.

She watched the girl and could picture herself doing it in her mind.

When she refocused back on reality, she heard the girl jump off her horse and start to come to the stables. Liza ran after her to see if the girl would tell her how she taught her horse to do the spin hop trick.

Liza caught up with the girl while cleaning up her horse's stall.

She asked, "Can I help you?"

The girl raised her eyebrow and said, "Sure, but I'm mucking out." She laughed, "I'm not sure how much you like doing those types of things."

Liza shrugged. "It's all part of having a horse," she laughed, "but it's definitely not the best part."

"I'm Cheri," the older girl said.

"I'm Liza," Liza replied, and she picked up a rake and started cleaning the stall with hay.

"Liza, thanks for your help! What can I do for you?" Cheri asked.

"Well, I saw that cute trick you did with your horse, and I was wondering how you taught him that?"

"Oh, that's easy!" Cheri said. She broke down the instructions and explained that treats were an amazing motivator.

"That sounds great," Liza said, smiling. "Thank you!"

Liza helped Cheri clean out her horse, Horatio's stall, and spent the rest of the day dreaming about how she would teach Candy to do the little skip and hop after her jump. Liza knew it was the best way to win the cup.

The next few days did not go well.

Liza fell off of Candy.

Candy did not want to make the motions Liza instructed.

Liza tripped over Candy.

Bad things just kept happening.

At the end of the third day, Liza decided that the silver cup was just not worth it this year. Candy was tired and acting stubborn, and Liza was sore and frustrated. Liza heard a familiar and friendly voice as she stomped into the stable with Candy.

"Hi, Liza! It's me, Cheri. Do you remember?" Cheri said as she stopped in front of Candy and Liza.

Liza nodded and gave Cheri a smile. It wasn't her fault that Candy and Liza couldn't do the trick. "Hi, Cheri—how are you doing?"

"Oh, I'm good. Just coming to see Horatio and find out what nonsense he's gotten up to while I was away." Cheri laughed then asked, "How are you and Candy doing with the new trick?"

Liza shrugged. She didn't really want to admit that the trick was a huge bust, especially because Cheri and Horatio did it so well. Still, Cheri seemed nice enough, and Liza decided to confide in her.

"I decided that we wouldn't add it to the other trick. It's a bit too much for Candy, at least right now. We just don't seem to be at the same level." Liza said. She was a bit disappointed but also didn't want to push Candy too far. Liza did not want to hurt her horse.

"Oh," Cheri said. She studied Liza for a moment. Liza wanted to run away from the judgment, but then Cheri said, "You know, it took Horatio and me a few weeks to get the trick right. It was just a weird movement for me to teach him. We kept having problems with it. I felt like we wouldn't be able to do it either, but then, one day, it just clicked because we kept it up."

Liza listened to everything Cheri said and shook her head in disbelief. "But you guys are so good at it."

"Now we are. We've been doing that trick for over a year. He loves doing it once he understands where to put his legs."

"Ooooh," Liza said as the lightbulb clicked on for her. "What problems did you have?"

"Well, I fell a lot. Horatio kept wanting to do other tricks, and there were even a few times where I felt he was pretty frustrated with me because he couldn't get the trick right either."

"That sounds familiar!" Liza laughed. It was nice knowing that Cheri had similar issues. However, Liza was glad Cheri didn't get hurt when she fell off Horatio.

"Wow. Thank you for sharing your story with me. I thought we didn't have the right skills to do the trick. But now that I know you had trouble at first, it makes me think I was giving up too quickly," Liza said.

"Any time! I've been watching you guys do jumps for a while. You and Candy have the right stuff to make the trick happen," Cheri reassured her.

Liza blushed and hugged Cheri. "Thank you for the compliment. I'm looking forward to trying again tomorrow."

"Sounds good; good luck! See you soon," Cheri said as she walked away.

Liza went home that night and planned how she would tackle the trick another time.

Throughout the next week and a half, Liza trained with Candy every day.

And soon, despite other bumps, bruises, and frustrating moments, Liza started to see that their practice was paying off.

The day of the tournament arrived, and Liza was nervous about doing her new trick with Candy. She knew they were ready.

They got ready, went out with the rest of her age group, and Liza watched as other kids on their horses did fun tricks and did them well. She noted that no one stepped up their competition and tried something new. That made Liza hopeful that things would go well for her.

When it was Liza's turn, she and Candy trotted around the ring for a few moments, then they took off running toward the jump. Candy leapt over the highest bar and landed with a quiet *thump.*

Liza then nudged her horse to do the spin one way, then spin another. She said, "Hup!" to encourage Candy to kick her back legs up. And Candy did.

Liza beamed, they finished the trick, and the crowd cheered for her.

As Liza and the other students sat on their horses in the ring and waited for the announcers to reveal who the winner of the trick competition was, Liza realized that she had already won. She overcame self-doubt and worry and completed a lot of hard work. So, no matter the outcome, she learned a lot in two weeks and was very proud of her and Candy. She turned her attention just in time to hear who the first-place winner was.

"The winner of the Silver Cup is . . . Liza and Candy!"

~ ~ ~

Make the impossible possible—there are many times that things feel impossible. But one thing to remind yourself is that very few things are impossible. Listen to what you want to do and keep moving toward it, even when your mind tells you you cannot. Most of the things in life are possible. You just have to find the right formula!

Darla the Team Player

There are many things in the world that you know, love, and care about. But do you know everything about them? Or can you find out more about the thing you love? You can always find a new way to do things.

The story below includes Darla, a girl who loves to play basketball. She loves it so much but thinks she doesn't have anything more to learn. What do you think happens to Darla when she finds out just how wrong she was and a new teammate shows her new things and new ways to play the game?

What would you do if you knew that someone knew more than you about a subject or activity you loved?

~ ~ ~

Darla closed her eyes.

Bump, bump, bump.

Darla listened to the rhythm of the basketball hitting the gymnasium court.

As the speed picked up, the rhythm picked up too.

Bump, bump, bump, ditty, bump.

Bump, bump, bump, ditty, bump.

Bump, bump, bump, ditty, bump.

Darla opened her eyes and moved her feet with the rhythm of the beat. She ran forward, shifted around a player, stepped back, and tossed the ball into the net.

Swish!

The ball bounced on the floor as Darla cheered.

"Darla, that wasn't the play you were supposed to do!" the coach called to her.

"Yeah, but I made the shot," Darla called back. She jogged over to the coach. "I made the point. That was what we were trying to do."

"No, Darla. There are no points in practice. You know this. I wanted you to be a team player and let the other members have a chance to do some drills. You are not part of a team right now. You're just doing what you want. You have to go sit on the bench for a penalty. If you did that in a game, a referee might do the same thing."

Darla crossed her arms over her chest and walked away. "That's because I'm doing what is best." Darla couldn't get the coach to understand that she lived for basketball. Each morning she woke up and did ten push-ups to strengthen her arms. She ate all the right foods. She practiced after school with the team and then went home and practiced more drills after dinner. Darla knew what she was doing. She just couldn't get the coach to see it.

As she plunked down onto the bench, she swiped a water bottle and squirted it into her mouth. She didn't want to just sit here. It was one of the worst things about having a penalty, the sitting, the waiting.

Coach Mitchell was wrong.

Penalties weren't given to players who made baskets. They were given to players who elbowed, tripped, hit, and started fights.

Darla muttered again, "I know what I'm doing."

After practice, Darla's mom talked with the coach for a long time. Darla grew even more impatient. She had already had to sit out for a lot during practice. Now the coach was ratting her out to her mom. Darla rolled her eyes at the thought.

As her mom walked over, she put a hand on her daughter's shoulder. "Come on, Darla. Let's go home."

Darla was a bit shocked when her mom didn't say anything about being benched for practice, but she was sure that she would hear more about it.

When Darla turned around to look at the coach, she saw a girl she didn't know walk up to him. She was doing a few dribbles Darla hadn't seen before, but the door closed before she could see what happened next.

In the car, Darla's mom sighed. "I think that as much as you love basketball, you're not learning some other lessons that go with it."

Darla's ears perked up. "What do you mean?"

"I mean, I have always taught you to be a kind person, but it doesn't seem like you are one when you are out on the court. Coach Mitchell said you were very rude to him today."

"I wasn't! He was rude to me. He benched me," Darla complained.

"Because you weren't being part of the team. You just did what you wanted to do," Darla's mom said.

"Yeah. Because I knew what would get us the points," Darla retorted.

"Basketball is more about points, Darla."

Darla harrumphed and slumped back in her seat. She didn't have anything more to say to her mom. She looked out the window, watched as the houses and trees went by, and listened to the sound of the tires on the road until they were home.

The next day at practice, Coach Mitchell gathered everyone up for a team huddle. Darla didn't think this was out of the ordinary because they huddled every time before a game or practice. What Darla did think was out of the ordinary was that the girl from yesterday was standing next to the coach with a basketball under her arm.

"Team, this is Samantha. She just moved here and would like to join. She showed me some of her moves yesterday and I think she has the right stuff. I'd like you to welcome her into practice today and let's show her what we are made of. Does that sound good?"

The girls cheered.

Darla did not.

She stared at the new girl, unsure of what to think.

On the court, Coach Mitchell gave Darla a different position than normal. Usually, she played as the point guard. Instead, he made her a power forward.

"Coach, I don't want to be a power forward. I want to be a point guard," she complained.

"I know. But we will try Samantha out in all positions to see where she is best at. This isn't a permanent switch. It's a try-out. I have to do what is best for the team."

Thinking about what her mother said, Darla bit her lip. She turned around and marched back to her new position. As the coach blew the whistle and the girls started to move around the court, Darla's anger subsided a little.

She was in awe of how Samantha moved and what she did.

Suddenly, Darla realized that Samantha was better at basketball than she was. Darla was shocked.

After practice, Darla was very impressed with how much Samantha knew. She was surprised by some of the moves and even some of the shots she made. Darla wasn't sure about what she had to do to improve herself, but if she didn't she would never be able to keep up with Samantha.

On the way home from practice, Darla asked her mom, "Mom, what do you do when someone is better than you at something?"

Darla's mom raised her eyebrows "Oh," she said, taking a moment to think, "Well, someone is always going to be better than you at something. Even the thing you like the most in the world. It's just the way it works. But, you can always strive to be better and learn more."

Darla nodded, deep in thought. "I guess I have to do that."

Darla thought all night and all day at school, but she wasn't sure how she would learn more about basketball than she already did.

Finally, she concluded that she would probably have to talk to the coach about it. As much as Darla didn't like admitting she didn't know what to do, especially to Coach Mitchell, he seemed as though he would be the right person to ask.

At least for a place to start.

Darla got to practice early to speak with the coach. She inhaled deeply and gulped down her nerves. She walked up to him and said, "I'd like to learn more about basketball so I can get to be as good as Samantha."

"Well, hello, Darla—how are you today?" Coach Mitchell said sarcastically.

Darla rolled her eyes. She knew Coach Mitchell was expressing that she wasn't being polite enough. "I'm just excited, and I am not trying to be rude. I am sorry for not asking how you are doing."

Coach Mitchell turned to Darla and said, "Thank you." He smiled at her. "It's nice to see that you're picking up on some cues now."

Darla let out a long exhale. "Samantha is better than me."

"I wouldn't say better, but she has different skills that you want."

"Okay, how do I get them?"

"Why don't you talk with Samantha? I think you girls could learn something from each other. You might even become friends," Coach suggested.

Darla nodded and said, "Thanks, Coach. I think you're right."

He chuckled. "If I had known that bringing another teammate in who would challenge you would excite you this much, I would have done it long ago." Coach Mitchell patted Darla on the back, "I'm glad to see you are so excited."

Darla found Samantha looking at a map of the school. She walked up and said, "Hi, do you need help? I'm Darla. I'm on your basketball team?"

Samantha smiled and said, "Yes, thank you. I'm looking for the library. Mrs. Olsen said that I could get some books for class there."

"It's this way. Follow me." Darla said, smiling. "You have Mrs. Olsen?"

"Yes, I met with her yesterday before practice."

"Neat. I do too! Maybe we'll be in the same class."

"Awesome!" Samantha grinned.

"Do you think we could play basketball sometime? I saw how great some of your moves and shots were, and I would love to learn more about them."

"Yes! Thank you. That sounds amazing." Samantha looked down at her shoes. "I think you have some great techniques I'd like to learn too. Want to get together after school?"

"Yes! That would be great," Darla said excitedly.

From that day forward, until Samantha and Darla no longer lived in the same town, they met after school to play basketball. And they stayed lifelong friends.

~ ~ ~

Never stop learning—whether you know it or not, each day you remember and learn a little more. In fact, you never stop learning. When you think you have all the information about a subject, understand that someone else will always know more. You can grow amazingly when you keep your mind open to new things. When you keep your mind open, you'll become better than you currently are.

Juniper Loves Her Teddy Bear

Every time we grow into a new phase of life, it seems as though there is something we might have to let go of. As you get older, you may stop playing with your toys and move on to other things that interest you more.

100

But the magic and love you add to the things you used to be attached to will never fade from your memory.

Sometimes it's hard to remember that letting go of one thing makes room for another, but that doesn't mean you'll forget the other things in your life that were once incredible. It means you'll have a chance to build more memories and grow into a new part of who you were always supposed to be.

Juniper is the last character we are going to read about. She is getting ready to go to school but doesn't want to let her teddy bear go. Instead, she tries to sneak Ivy away to school with her, but with a dream and a little encouragement from her dad, she realizes that there are times when she has to let go.

What do you think Ivy says to Juniper to know it's okay? Have you had to be brave and try something new as you grew older?

~ ~ ~

"Dad, I can't find my book bag," Juniper called down the hall. "I want to make sure that I have everything for first grade."

"Juniper, sweetie. We packed your bag yesterday. We double-checked it today. We don't need to check it again. Okay? It's time to go to bed," her dad replied.

Juniper bit her lip. She knew they had checked and double-checked her book bag, but she wanted to put one more thing inside it. Her mom had told her that other kids in her class wouldn't be bringing their stuffed animals. Although Juniper chose not to bring Ivy her teddy bear, she was having second thoughts.

Juniper knew that her parents would let her bring it if she wanted to, at least in her book bag, but she didn't want them to know she had changed her mind. Something about taking a teddy bear to first grade made her feel embarrassed, but she wasn't sure why. She knew that sneaking Ivy into her book bag was the right choice.

That would make her feel less nervous about going to school all day. Ivy always made her feel better.

As her nerves pricked at her chest, Juniper picked Ivy up. She cradled the fuzzy bear inside one arm and played with the hem of Ivy's dress between two of her fingers. It was a habit Juniper had picked up long before she could remember. The hem had a spot where the design had worn away because Juniper had rubbed it so much, but that only seemed to make the silky spot even softer. Ivy, also had soft and plushy, brown fur. Juniper loved rubbing Ivy's ears to help her fall asleep at night.

"Juniper, it's time to get ready for bed. Are your teeth brushed?" Juniper's mom asked.

"No."

"Do you have your pajamas on?" Juniper's mom continued.

"No."

"Do you have your school clothes ready for tomorrow?"

Juniper looked back at her dresser. She had a sock and a shirt out but had forgotten to pull out the rest of her school clothes. "Sorta."

Juniper's mom smiled. "Don't you think we should do all of those things before you go to bed then?"

"Yes," Juniper reluctantly agreed.

"Well, you have to put Ivy down first."

Knowing that she wasn't going to be with her for a long time tomorrow, Juniper did not like the idea of putting Ivy down, but she did anyway. She placed her stuffed bear on her bed, kissed Ivy's cheek, and whispered, "I'll be back very soon."

Juniper then rushed to get ready for bed.

She brushed her teeth.

She put on her pajamas.

She picked out the rest of her clothes to wear tomorrow.

Then she climbed into bed next to Ivy. As her mom and dad kissed her good night, she snuggled into her pillows. Juniper began to dream.

In her dream, Juniper ran along a path of pink clouds with Ivy. Everything smelled like cotton candy, and the birds were singing her favorite song.

Juniper laughed as she bounced high into the sky and fell back down to the cloud. She jumped again, and her hair flew away from her face, and as she landed, she shook it back into place.

Ivy rolled off the pink cloud and giggled at Juniper. She shook off the clouds in her fur and brushed the parts of her dress that collected the willow wisps on them.

"Oh!" Juniper said, "Ivy! I have so much to tell you about."

"Juniper, I have things to tell you too," the bear's stitched mouth opened in Juniper's dreamland. "Let's go to our special tree. We can eat candy apples and gummy worms, then tell each other all our secrets."

Juniper and Ivy skipped to their favorite spot in their dream world. They held hands and made each other laugh along the way by rolling and tumbling. Each time their feet hit the cloud path, a small piece would tuft and fly into the sky. Each tuft smelled a little different, but each scent was one of Juniper and Ivy's favorite smells. Strawberries, lilacs, cotton candy, and more.

When they reached their favorite tree, Juniper picked some red candied apples and pulled out a few extra gummy worms from the tree because they were the best candy, according to Ivy. Ivy sat on the ground with her black button eyes blinking. She couldn't help Juniper because she was too small, but she offered good support (at least that's what Ivy thought).

Juniper jumped down the tree and sat next to Ivy. She handed her teddy bear many gummy worms and munched on a candied apple. "You tell me what you want to first," Juniper said to Ivy.

"Well," Ivy said, swallowing a gummy worm, "This is very important, and I don't think we should have candy in our mouths when we do it."

Juniper sat up and said, "Oh."

Juniper swallowed the bite of the apple she had just taken and looked at Ivy. "Is everything okay?"

Ivy pushed herself up with her stuffed arms and stuffed legs and wobbled over to Juniper. Ivy looked at Juniper and said, "You are growing up. You need to go to first grade without me. I will be okay. You will be okay. We will still be together when you get home. I'll still sleep with you and we can still play, but this is an important step."

Juniper teared up at the thought. "But I love you."

"I love you too! Going to first grade isn't going to change how much we love each other, is it?" Ivy asked.

Juniper shook her head and said, "No."

"Right! So just try it. For two days. If you don't like being at school without me, I'll come with you, okay?" The bear promised.

Juniper sniffled. "Okay. That sounds like a good plan."

"Good! Let's finish eating this candy before it's time to wake up!"

Juniper smiled. Ivy always knew how to make Juniper feel better.

In the morning, Juniper woke up. She hugged Ivy and said, "Thank you. That was a really good talk last night."

Juniper dressed, ate breakfast, brushed her teeth, and put her book bag on her back.

For the briefest moment, she thought about running upstairs again just to stuff Ivy into her backpack but remembered their agreement. "Two days," Juniper whispered to herself.

Then she walked through the door without second thoughts.

When Juniper returned from school, she raced up the stairs to talk with Ivy. She had missed Ivy very much and was happy that Ivy got to spend her day out of the book bag. Juniper wouldn't have had time to spend with Ivy when she was at school because she was so busy.

"Ivy! I have so much to tell you! You were right about school. But I'm so glad to see you."

Juniper hugged her teddy bear and started telling Ivy all about her day.

From that day forward, Ivy stayed on Juniper's bed while she was at school and Juniper would come home to tell her about her day.

It was an amazing new routine for a great new phase in Juniper's life.

~ ~ ~

There are things and people you love very much, and they love you too! But, at certain times, especially growing up, you must step away from the people and things you love the most. It doesn't mean you don't love them as much as you did. It means that you are finding new ways to enjoy life and be independent. Those people and things will be there when you get back, and they will be happy that you stepped into a new adventure.

Epilogue

Think about all the characters you read about today. How are they like you? How are they different? What would you do if you were in their situation?

How do you treat yourself when you are feeling happy, sad, angry, mad, content, or any other emotion? How you treat yourself mirrors how you treat the rest of the world. Make sure to approach any problems, feelings, and challenges without judgment.

When you approach challenges with love, compassion, and kindness, you're spreading the light you have inside of you to your corner of the world. Your light will shine onto others and inspire them to spread their light, and then soon after, so many people will be encouraged that their light will come back and shine on you.

Remember that even your dreams can inspire. Follow them to the fullest, work as hard as you can, and spread your inspiration to others. When you infuse the right balance of being true to your beliefs, views, and kindness and you follow even your biggest dreams, you can create a beautiful life and show everyone in your world how amazing you truly are.

Bonuses

Our Gifts For You

Subscribe to our Newsletter and receive these free materials

 Scan Me

www.specialartbooks.com/free-materials/

Stay Connected with Us

Instagram: @specialart_coloring
Facebook Group: Special Art - Kids Entertainment
Website: www.specialartbooks.com

Impressum

For questions, feedback, and suggestions:

support@specialartbooks.com

Nadia Ross, Special Art

Copyright © 2022

www.specialartbooks.com

Images by © Shutterstock

Cover Illustration realized by
Maria Francesca Perifano

Printed in Great Britain
by Amazon

23073432R00066